W9-CPE-516

The Star Counters

BY IDA LUTTRELL

PICTURES BY KORINNA PRETRO

TAMBOURINE BOOKS  NEW YORK

NORTHPORT PUBLIC LIBRARY
NORTHPORT, NEW YORK

Long ago there lived a king so greedy and selfish that he made everyone else miserable. The king owned mountains and trees, valleys and seas, and all the stars in the sky...or so he thought.

Since the stars were bright and shiny the king was certain that they were made of pure gold.

"What if a thief takes one?" he fretted. "I will count them every night to make sure none are missing."

That night the king began to count the stars. He started in the east and counted toward the west. Intent on numbers, the king failed to see a shooting star, the moon's soft radiance, or other splendors of the night. As dawn approached he was still counting.

"Nine billion and seven, nine billion and eight, and the last star, nine billion and nine!"

The king fell to the ground exhausted. He slept all day and arose determined to find a star counter.

Soon he came upon a turtle plodding down the road. The turtle stopped for a column of ants to cross his path. To the king's surprise and delight, the turtle began to count.

"One, two, three, four ..."

"You there, Turtle," said the king, "I have a job for you."

So Turtle became Star Counter of the Universe. And the king went to bed happy.

The next morning he rushed out to the courtyard. He found Turtle fast asleep.

"Wake up!" the king shouted. "How many stars did you count?"

"Ten," said Turtle, and he blinked and smiled proudly.

"Ten!" the king roared. "There are nine billion and nine stars in my sky and you only counted ten?"

"Yes," said Turtle. "I can only count to ten."

"Worthless dolt!" said the king. And he locked Turtle under the royal kitchen and made him drink dishwater.

The king set out again to find a star counter. He stopped to rest beside a pond and saw a vain fox admiring himself in the water.

The fox began to brush his tail.

"What a beautiful tail I have," he said. "It is thicker than that of any fox in the kingdom."

And to make sure, he counted the hairs in his tail.

The king watched and listened as the fox counted.

"One million and one, one million and two..."

"A perfect star counter," the king said. "Fox, consider yourself lucky. I have chosen you to count my stars."

So Fox counted stars when they came out that night. He found it easier than counting hairs because the stars were bright and beautiful. And some were larger than the others. But this troubled Fox.

"The brightest stars are more beautiful than I," Fox thought, and he refused to count them.

The king rose with the sun and raced to the courtyard, his nightcap still on his head.

"How many stars?" he asked.

"Nine billion and one," said Fox.

"What!" cried the king. "Eight stars are missing. What have you done with them?"

Clever Fox quickly added the numbers together, counting on his knees and elbows, feet and toes.

"Nine billion and nine," cried Fox, "is what I meant to say."

"Impudent wretch!" shouted the king. "Do you think I would fall for such trickery?" And he locked Fox in a tower and made him eat boiled buzzard feathers.

Once more the king looked for a star counter. He had gone no further than the meadow surrounding the castle when he saw a cow resting under a tree. He heard the cow count as she chewed her cud.

"One billion and one times, one billion and two times, one billion and three times, and swallow."

"Wonderful," said the king. "Cow, come with me. You are to stay awake all night and count every star in the sky."

"The moon too?" asked Cow, for she took pride in doing a job well.

"No," snapped the king, "only the stars."

Cow loved the stars so she was happy to take on the task. That night she climbed a nearby hill and counted every star, except the shooting stars that seemed to come from nowhere and then disappear. When she had counted five billion and five, she went to drink from a pond in the meadow. Refreshed, she returned to her hill and counted the rest.

At daybreak the king dashed out, his nightshirt flying.

"How many?" he asked, all out of breath.

"I counted nine billion and nine," said Cow.

"Splendid!" cried the king, and he gave Cow all the hay she could eat.

Night after night Cow counted stars, drank from the pond in the meadow, and counted stars again. Sometimes she sang or made verses about the stars as she counted them. During the day she ate and slept.

The king was quite happy with this arrangement for a time. But he noticed Cow becoming fat. The king wondered if Cow indeed counted the stars every night. Or did she eat and sleep instead and tell him "nine billion and nine" every morning?

The king wondered and worried until nightfall. Then he hid himself in the greenery on the hill and watched Cow. As the stars came out, Cow began to count.

The king watched her count to five billion and five. Then Cow got up and started down the hill to the meadow.

"Aha!" the king said to himself. "Trickery is afoot."

He kept to the shadows and followed Cow to the
pond, where stars glittered on the water.

Cow took a drink, rippling the water and causing the
stars to dance crazily around her mouth.

The king leaped from his hiding place and screamed,
"You are swallowing my stars! You shall pay dearly for
this. Guards, seize her!" The king bellowed so hard
he lost his footing, fell in the pond, and thrashed about
crying, "Help me!"

Kind, forgiving Cow jumped in and heaved him from the pond. The king stumbled to his feet in time to see a shower of shooting stars burst across the sky.

"My stars are falling," the crazed king shrieked. "I must find them, every one." And he raced across the meadow, over the hill, and out of the kingdom, never to be seen again.

Everyone celebrated, even the guards.

They set Turtle and Fox free and
awarded Cow a garland of flowers.

As for the stars, they remain in the sky for all to enjoy. Though some say, on soft summer nights, in meadows where cows rest, you can see stars sparkle in the tall grass.

To Lauren Jane with love
I. L.

To my dear grandnephews Ivan, Sergey, and Theodor
K. P.

Text copyright © 1994 by Ida Luttrell · Illustrations copyright © 1994 by Korinna Pretro
All rights reserved. No part of this book may be reproduced or utilized in any form or by any means, electronic or mechanical, including photocopying, recording, or by any information storage or retrieval system, without permission in writing from the Publisher. Inquiries should be addressed to Tambourine Books, a division of William Morrow & Company, Inc., 1350 Avenue of the Americas, New York, New York 10019.

Printed in Singapore

Library of Congress Cataloging in Publication Data

Luttrell, Ida. The star counters/by Ida Luttrell; illustrated by Korinna Pretro.— 1st ed. p. cm.
Summary: Believing that he owns the stars, a greedy king hires several animals to count them each night.
[1. Stars—Fiction.   2. Greed—Fiction.   3. Kings, queens, rulers, etc.—Fiction.   4. Counting.
5. Animals—Fiction.]   I. Pretro, Korinna, ill.   II. Title.
PZ7.L97953St1994 [E]—dc20   93-20342 CIP AC
ISBN 0-688-12149-7.—ISBN 0-688-12150-0 (lib. bdg.)
1 3 5 7 9 10 8 6 4 2
First edition